THE TROUBLE WITH PIXIES

(Edinburgh Elementals)

By Gayle Ramage

Michael paused at the bottom of the staircase, one hand gripped on to mahogany banister as he looked upwards. Having just lugged the last of the boxes up the first set of stairs, bound for his new bedroom, he was now ready to relax. But he'd heard something, like the low murmuring of distant voices. He remained still and listened for more noises but all was silent. The place was old, built in the Georgian era when Edinburgh decided it needed to have more houses to the north of the city, and was thus dubbed the New Town. It could have been the piping he'd heard, or just the natural groan of an ageing building. Putting it from his mind, he headed to the kitchen and poured himself a glass of red wine. He had intended to unpack the few remaining boxes left from the move up to the scottish capital from Norfolk, but he could deal with that tomorrow. What he needed was a nice, relaxing drink while the kids, led by Michael's eldest - seventeen-year-old Tom - were out exploring the city.

Michael had just sat down on the black leather sofa he'd brought up from the old house, when there came a sharp rap at the front door. With a heavy sigh, he put the untouched drink on the mantelpiece and went to see who was paying a visit. Pulling the door open, he was met with a black-and-white woollen deerstalker; the large white bobble inches from his face. Its wearer was peering down into a multicoloured rucksack.

'Hi, Elsa. Sorry I'm a couple of months later,' said the hat with a feminine Scottish burr. 'Should have rang to say I was coming back today. Can I have my key, please?' When Michael only responded with a frown, the hat moved upwards to reveal its wearer; a small, pale-faced woman with two different-coloured eyes, one violet, the other green. A smattering of freckles lay across the bridge of her nose and a couple of strands of red hair appeared to have escaped the clutches of the hat. 'You're not Elsa,' she said, with a hint of suspicion. She peered over his shoulder as if expecting someone to be standing in the hallway. 'Where is she?'

'I don't know, I'm afraid.'

'Afraid?' She leapt on the word like an interrogator leaping on a random word. 'Why?'

'Oh. Sorry, I meant I don't know anyone called Elsa,' Michael explained. 'Unless you're referring to the lady that used to live here. I never found out her first name.'

'*Used* to live here?'

'I believe she passed away about three months ago.' Michael was prevented from saying any more by the woman gripping his arm; her face ashen.

'O gods,' she muttered. 'O gods, O gods, O gods. How did she die? Please, it's very important.'

'I - I was told it was natural causes. Died in her sleep. Peaceful,' he blustered.

The woman had been holding her breath as she'd listened to Michael. Now she exhaled slowly, and released his arm. 'Well, that's something,' she said, heavily.

'Look, I feel awful for being the one to break the news about your friend,' said Michael. 'I was just about to have a quiet glass of wine. You're more than welcome to join me. You look like you need a drink.'

She glanced behind her for a moment, then faced Michael again and nodded. 'That would be lovely. Thank you.'

He stood aside to admit her and realised there were several various-sized rucksacks and backpacks by her feet. Instantly, he took as many he could carry and brought them inside, casting an eye at the grey clouds overhead, leaving her to carry the smaller bag in. With the bags sitting in the hallway, he showed her through to the living room then dashed back through to the kitchen to retrieve another wine glass. When he returned, the woman was stood by the unlit fireplace, taking in the room and sipping from the glass of wine Michael had put down to answer the door.

'Looks totally different,' she said, nodding at the sparse furniture and decor adorning the spacious room.

'It was pretty bare when we moved in,' Michael explained, pouring himself another glass from the bottle on the coffee table. 'A couple of bits of furniture, that's all. I think Elsa's family must have taken the rest, or sold it.'

The woman rolled her eyes. 'I think they would have sold Elsa herself if they'd got a good deal out of it.'

'Ah.'

'She always used to say that she was sure she'd brought home the wrong babies from the hospital. And if she didn't, then she sure as hell wished she had."

Michael laughed. 'Sounds like she was quite the woman.'

'Yes, she was,' the odd-eyed woman said softly.

Another sip of the wine seemed to perk her up. 'Anyway, a strange woman shows up on your doorstep, drinks your wine, and doesn't even have the manners to introduce herself.' She moved towards him, extending her free hand. 'I'm Hattie.'

Her hand felt surprisingly warm to the touch. 'Nice to meet you. I'm Michael.'

Introductions made, Hattie took a comfortable step back and smiled genially at him. 'So, is it just yourself here, or are your family about to jump out and say "boo"?'

'Well, I do have a family. Three kids. They're out exploring the city.' Michael replied, beckoning Hattie to take the seat by the fireplace. He sat back down on the sofa. 'I was a bit wary of letting them out in a new city but my eldest is mature enough to look after the others. Well, I like to think he's mature, anyway.' He stared at his drink for a moment. 'He's got his mobile phone so he's just a call or text away.'

'Exactly,' agreed Hattie. 'Explored the house yet?'

Michael shook his head and took another sip of wine. 'I think I'll leave that for tomorrow. We left the old house just before seven this morning so I'm too tired to do an Indiana Jones at the moment. Actually, once the kids get back, I'll get Ben and Ingrid settled and get some sleep myself.'

'Is that a subtle hint that you want me to go?' Hattie asked, a smile flickering on the edge of her mouth.

'Oh goodness, no,' Michael said, not meaning to cause any offence.

Hattie's smiled widened and she placed her empty glass on the coffee table. 'Don't worry about it. I'm quite tired myself. It'll be nice to sleep in my own bed again.' She got to her feet again and Michael did likewise, placing his own glass next to hers.

'Yes,' said Michael, following Hattie through to the front door. 'There's nothing like your own bed. Did you stay in many hotels while you were away?'

'Pah!' Hattie erupted. 'Hotels? I wish!' Michael expected her to continue, explain her words, but she started picking up her bags instead.

'Do you want help with these?' he asked, already lifting a paisley-patterned carpet bag which smelt distinctly of lavender and iron.

'Thanks,' she replied, awkwardly opening the door handle with her elbow. 'I live in the house opposite so it's not too far.'

Michael managed to grab hold of another bag, a small suitcase this time, before Hattie disappeared into the cold darkening sky outside. Three bags still remained in the hallway but he could nip back to get them in a minute.

There was an abandoned coldness about Hattie's house that made Michael shiver almost as soon as he'd stepped over the threshold. But it was to be expected if the owner had been away for over four months. The place was in darkness. Hattie tried the light switch nearest the door but nothing happened.

'The meter's obviously run out of juice,' she explained, not sounding too bothered by the fact. 'I'll sort it out tomorrow.'

'Will you be all right without any power?' he asked, looking around the gloomy hallway where the only visible thing was the wooden flooring and the corner of a side table.

Hattie swept the small pile of mail which had accumulated on the doormat during her absence, and nodded. 'I'm used to it,' she said, with a shrug. 'Thanks for the help,' she said, facing him with a smile.

'That's quite all right. There's still a couple of bags in my hallway. I'll be right back.' Turning, he walked hurriedly back to his house and returned less than a minute later carrying the rest of Hattie's things. He set them down in the hallway with a groan. 'My goodness, what have you got in these things?' he asked, feeling a twinge in his back as he straightened up.

'Oh, just the usual,' Hattie replied, a little too breezily. 'Thanks once again.'

'No problem. And if you need anything, you know where we are.'

Hattie smiled again. 'Shouldn't I be saying that to you, you being the newcomer?'

'It works both ways,' Michael replied, diplomatically. He turned to head through the open door again.

'Enjoy your exploration day tomorrow,' Hattie said, standing with one hand leaning against the door frame. 'You'll have been told about the attic, I assume.'

This made Michael pause. He stopped walking and turned to face her. 'The attic? Why?'

'Michael, has anyone been up in the attic?' she asked in a controlled voice.

'Just my son, Ben.' He faltered, seeing the alarmed expression forming quickly on her face as she rushed past him, leaving her door wide open. Ever the cautious person, he closed her door and ran after her as she burst into his house. By the time he reached the hallway, his neighbour was nowhere to be seen, although the heavy sound of someone running up the winding staircase alerted him to where she was. Slamming his own front door closed, he gave chase, reaching the top of the second set of stairs to catch his breath. Hattie was standing by the door to the attic, both hands grasping the round door handle and making sure the room stayed closed. 'What's going on?' Michael said finally, feeling a slight tightening in his chest. He looked across at the woman. She was glaring back at him accusingly.

'Some idiot opened this door, that's what's going on,' she hissed.

'My son was the one who opened the attic door, and he is by no means an idiot. Why don't you want anyone going in there? My kids never found anything strange about it. In fact, my son wants it to be his bedroom - once we get repairs made, of course.'

Hattie looked at him in disbelief. 'And you don't mind your son sharing a room with -' She broke off and lunged forward, grabbing him by the arm and pulling him towards her.

'Sharing a room with what? What are you doing?' Michael insisted, trying to keep his cool, despite the increasingly bizarre turn of events. But Hattie wasn't listening. She took hold of his hands and placed them over the handle, warning him to keep the door closed no matter what, before storming down the stairs again. 'Where are you going now?' Michael yelled.

'Back in a second,' she called back as if she was just popping out to the shops.

Michael waited a few seconds, hands still clamped around the door handle, before calling out for the woman again. 'Hattie!' No answer. He stared at the door frame, parts of the red paint peeling away. What was so terrible about the room beyond? Sure, the estate agent hadn't shown him this part of the house but only due to lack of a key, which he'd been subsequently sent after buying the place. Right now, he was tempted to throw the door open, if only for a second, just to see. See what, he wasn't sure. After all, the kids hadn't noticed anything odd when they'd been in there, earlier. And if they had, nothing had been mentioned.

On Hattie's reappearance, Michael was ready to demand she tell him what the heck was going on. But the sight of the thing in her hand shut him up. On first sight, he thought it was a gun and he would have automatically put up his hands in a surrendering mode, but as she approached him he realised it wasn't quite like a normal gun. Not that he'd seen many in real life.

'Okay,' Hattie said, exhaling sharply. 'You can let go of the handle, now.'

'Not until you explain exactly what's going on,' Michael said, firmly. 'I mean it. I don't know who you are. You could be anyone.'

'You think I'm nuts.' She said, and rolled her eyes.

'Quite frankly I'm not sure what to think. But all I know is neither of us are moving from this spot until everything is explained.'

'You won't believe me.'

'I'll be the judge of that.'

The stand-off continued a little while longer as Hattie stared at Michael. He just returned the gesture, adamant he, nor she, was going nowhere. Finally, her shoulders sagged and she gave in. 'Elsa had a spot of trouble with -' She stopped and narrowed her eyes. 'With some irritants, let's just say. She called on me and I contained them in this attic and locked the door. Elsa was under strict instructions never to unlock it unless I was present. But, of course, she went and died.'

'What do you mean by "irritants"?' Michael asked. 'Thieves? Trespassers? What?'

Hattie laughed bitterly. 'If it was that simple, the police would have been called straight away. No, these things needed a specialist.'

Michael frowned. Specialist? What, was she implying she was some sort of MI5 agent, or suchlike? Granted, the secret service probably recruited people who could blend seamlessly into society, not be noticed. With her different-coloured eyes and red hair tucked under that winter hat, she definitely stood out. 'You mean to tell me you're some kind of James Bond spy?'

She gave him a look as if she'd just realised he's crazy.

'Um, no,' she said carefully. 'Not exactly.'

Michael was getting sick of beating about the bush. 'Just tell me, then!' he shouted.

'They're pixies!' she screamed back.

The ensuing silence was deafening. Michael broke it by laughing. 'Pixies? What?'

Hattie shot him a scathing look, and Michael was sure her violet eye flashed momentarily in the dim glow of the lightbulb above them. 'Yes, Pixies. And if you'd ever had run-ins with them before, you would not be mocking me.'

'Well, I'm sorry but pixies?'

'Yes, yes. Pixies, pixies. That's what I said,' Hattie retorted, evidently getting just a little tired of Michael's reaction to the news of just what was in his attic space.

'So you locked pixies in my attic?' Michael said in confirmation. Despite his dubious tone, he still had his hands clamped to the door handle.

Hattie took off her hat, hung it over the bannister and ran a hand through her mane of curly red hair. Michael was momentarily taken aback by the abundance of hair which trailed down to her waist. It put him in mind of those pre-raphaelite paintings. It took Hattie to cough purposefully to make Michael realise he'd been staring. 'Could you stand aside, please?' she said, pressing a button on the gun-like weapon in her hand. It made a sound like it was charging up. Michael felt uneasy about having a dangerous thing like that in the home, but if he had been really worried, he would be frog-marching this strange woman down the stairs and out of the house. Hesitating for only a moment, he did as she asked and reluctantly stepped away from the door, worried but curious as to what would happen when she opened the attic door to find nothing in there. 'Okay,' she said, her voice calmer now. 'I'm going to count to three and then I'm going to open this door. Whatever you do, don't come into the room. You can stand in the doorway, just in case I need your help. All right?'

'Fine.'

She nodded and stood in front of the door, one hand on the door knob, the other grasping the weapon tightly. 'One... Two...' she whispered, 'THREE!' On the third count, she shoved open the door with enough violence for Michael to take a safe step back, and stalked into the room. The attic was almost pitch-black, save for the lights of the city casting a soft glow into the room. Michael was just about to reach for the light switch, but Hattie got there before him.

Despite his growing sense of Hattie being seriously mad, Michael did scan the room for anything out of the ordinary and felt a little ridiculous at the relief he felt when all he saw nothing but a bare, wooden floor and blank walls. He looked at Hattie, ready to tell her he told her so but she was aiming the weapon at a spot next to the window.

'What are you still doing here?' she asked in a cold voice.

'Sorry?' said Michael, unsure whether to step into the room.

As if not hearing him, she continued. 'The door's been unlocked. Why didn't you escape, huh?'

'There's nobody here, Hattie,' Michael said.

'Michael, come in and close the door. Stand guard against it,' she ordered, never taking her eyes away from the space. 'If you feel something try to open it, keep it closed.'

'What something? These pixies of yours? Well, I can't see them.'

At this, Hattie turned her head to glare at him. 'Well, of course you can't. You see my eyes? See how they're different colours? Well, regard them as being like 3D glasses.'

'3D glasses?'

'Yes. When things - creatures, like these pixies - want to become invisible to the naked human eye, only people with eyes like mine can still see them properly.' She paused. 'Okay, the 3D analogy was a bit crap but you understand what I'm saying?'

'I think so,' said Michael, thinking he did nothing of the kind.

'Good. So, please. Just do as I ask?'

Wordlessly, Michael stepped into the attic and closed the door, with his back against it.

'Thank you,' said Hattie, with what sounded like a little sigh.

'Now what?' Michael asked.

'Now,' Hattie answered, her fingers tightening their grip on the weapon. 'I'll do what I should have done months ago.'

'You're not going to kill them?'

'Of course not. Why would I do that? What a silly question,' she replied, making him feel utterly chastised for asking in the first place.

'Well what are you going to do?'

A smile appeared on her face. 'I'm going to paint them.'

And there it was. There was the signal that things had definitely become stranger. Michael didn't even bother asking what she meant by "paint them". He was learning fast that this appeared to be a relatively normal thing for his new neighbour to do. And here Michael thought his neighbours back in Norfolk were odd because of their obsession with toads; everything from toad patterned curtains (in all rooms) to embalmed toads kept in a trophy cupboard. They were normal compared to this.

When the first shot occurred, Michael realised what was different about the gun. It was the kind you got at those Paintball places. So that's what she meant, he thought, staring at the blue paint now splattered on the wall and half the window.

'Missed,' Hattie muttered, spinning round to aim at the far corner of the room. She fired again and another dollop of blue hit the attic wall. Michael winced and then leant forward slightly, peering at what looked like a small hand and wrist, all in blue, darting across to the other corner.

'Ha!' Hattie exclaimed, the gun still trained on the seemingly hovering hand. She pulled the trigger again and this time the paint revealed the rest of the creature. It never stopped long enough for Michael to get a good look at it, but the pixie, as Hattie had said, was at least three foot and painfully thin. 'One down, four to go,' said Hattie, her sights now on one of the remaining invisible creatures.

'There's five of them?' Michael asked, in a surprised tone. 'There's five pixies in my attic?' He knew how ridiculous he sounded but this whole evening was turning out to be a ridiculous farce, anyway.

'Not for long,' Hattie said. The gun went off again. Success first time. The pixie that had been scrambling across the sloping ceiling, fell to the floor with a thud and covered in blue. It lay there, making incoherent noises, though Michael was sure he heard the odd swear word coming from the throaty voice.

She caught another one pretty soon after. This one got hit full in the face. Grumbling, it went to join its blue-armed companion. To Michael it seemed as if the paint had some sort of mild tranquilizer mixed into it, to make the pixies give up once they were caught.

'Hedgehog!' Hattie barked, spinning round with her gun momentarily aimed at Michael. He jerked out of her range, puzzled at what she'd just said. But a moment later, he found a small, brown hedgehog nudging against his feet. Michael felt somewhat relieved at something <u>normal</u> being in the attic. Though quite why a small woodland creature would be running around in the top of a three-storey, urban dwelling, he couldn't possibly say.

'Don't let the bugger out,' Hattie said, aiming the gun at the thing which seemed to sense the danger it was in and desperately tried to push against Michael's feet.

'Jesus, you can't do that to a hedgehog!' Michael exclaimed, bending down to carefully lift the quivering animal up, making sure not to brush against the sharp quills. Holding it in his arms like the times he held his children as babies, Michael looked up to discover the gun was still trained on the hedgehog and himself. 'Seriously, what has he done to you?'

A red eyebrow rose for a moment then fell. 'Seriously, put the hedgehog down. Unless you want to be covered in blue paint, that is.' Hattie replied.

'Why?'

She gave him a hard glare and then drooped slightly. 'Because pixies can turn into hedgehogs when they feel they're in danger, or just want to go unobserved by humans.' She held up a hand before he could speak. 'Don't ask me why hedgehogs. I haven't got a clue. I'm not some walking encyclopedia of supernatural creatures, you know.'

Michael looked down at the hedgehog who stared back up at him with dark, beady eyes. He held the thing close, unsure whether to believe Hattie's words. That was until the hedgehog let out a distinct cackle. Michael threw the hedgehog from his arms and in mid-flight, the creature got barraged with the ammo of paint. Once it hit the floor, it made to run to the safety of the corner of the attic again but only took a few steps before seeming to give up and lay down for a sleep.

Time seemed to pass quickly as Hattie took down the rest of the pixies. Michael wasn't sure if the minutes had really flown by or if it was because he'd been caught up in the whole scenario. Nevertheless, soon a small cluster of blue sat despondently in the centre of the room. Occasionally, the hovering blue hand gave Hattie and Michael a gesture which Michael assumed was supposed to be rude. Hattie flicked her hair out of her eyes and beamed at Michael. 'All done,' she said brightly, throwing him the paintball gun which he caught one-handed.

'Now what?' he asked, afraid she was just going to leave them there.

'Now this,' she replied, digging a hand into her jacket pocket and fishing out what looked like a small ball of silver wiring. Whatever it was, it had all five pixies staring at it with alarm, though none, Michael noted, scrambled to get away from it. 'Unbreakable chain. Once this is used to tie someone up then they can't escape. Doesn't matter if they use the sharpest axe in the world to chop it, or a small explosive. Only the person who does the tying up can untie it again. Again, don't ask me how it works exactly.'

Michael thought it sounded horrendous as various images flashed before him, but he did not air his views.

'It's very rare and not many people have access to these,' she said as she slowly unwound the chain. 'I've only got it as I can be trusted not to misuse it.' There was a hint of pride about her voice. As she made the pixies and hedgehog stand up in a line, Michael watched her, holding the paintball gun at arm's length. She carefully started winding the wiring around the group, tightening it only enough for the creatures not to escape.

'Does the paint come off?' Michael asked, as she tied the wiring into a double-knot.

She glanced at him briefly. 'Of course it does. The poor things don't want to be constantly visible to others now, do they? Once I find out why they came to the city in the first place, I'll drive them down to Devon, to the countryside, where they belong.' She frowned. 'I'll have to stop off at a petrol station on my way there. Don't want to the car to conk out and have to explain myself to the AA.'

'You're letting them go?' said Michael, feeling a little confused.

Satisfied, the creatures couldn't escape, Hattie stood up and faced Michael. 'Well, I don't have any right to keep them or whatever you were thinking.'

'So you're not some sort of,' he paused, trying to find the right word, 'law enforcement officer for pixies?' He could see she was trying not to laugh. 'Well what are you, then?' he asked, slightly rattled at her reaction.

'Human. Just like you are.'

'But you know about pixies.'

'And the rest.'

'The rest?'

She nodded. 'Pixies are just one of a thousands of creatures out there that most humans can't normally see.' She explained. 'And they're just pranksters, the pixies. Harmless, really. It's the Ice Giants in the Highlands or -'

'Ice Giants? What?'

Hattie placed a hand on her hip, and looked at Michael pointedly. 'Are you just going to repeat everything I say?'

Michael thought about this. 'Quite possibly,' he answered.

'Look, all you have to know is that all those supposed mythical creatures that you heard or read about as a child, they're real. They're as real as you and me.'

'And you're someone who can see these creatures and protect us - humans, I mean - from them?'

She smiled. 'God, no. Well, not exactly. I'm not some superhero or anything. I've not got any special powers or magical swords. Sometimes humans can come up against the creatures but more often than not, it's creature against creature. Actually, I've just come back from spending six months with the Ice Giants helping them find somewhere to live, out of the way of humans.'

'Why you?' Michael asked. 'Is it only you? Or are there others like you, that can see these creatures?'

Hattie shrugged. 'No idea. I think there's still some out there. There must be, come to think of it, or I'd always be asked to go to this place or that place. And why me, you ask? Why not? As I said before, due to these babies -' She pointed up at her eyes. '- I can see these creatures. So I can help them.'

Michael stared down at the floor, shaking his head. 'This is a lot to take in.'

'Then don't,' Hattie told him. She stepped forward and placed a gentle hand on his shoulder. 'No one's asking you to. Just go back to your wine and your children and forget this ever happened.'

'I... I don't think I can,' he said honestly, looking into those strange eyes of hers. She stared back for a moment and then beamed, giving his shoulder a squeeze.

'Great! Then you won't mind me calling on your help now and again,' she said, happily. She sauntered back over to the pixies and lifted up the end of the wiring, keeping a tight grasp of it as she started pulling the group forward.

'Hang on, what do you mean "my help"?' Michael asked, with a frown.

She stopped in front of him, the little band of visible pixie body parts stopping inches from her. 'Oh, you know - looking after my house if I'm called away, picking up my post. That kind of thing.' She regarded him with a smile. 'Why, did you think I meant something else? You did, didn't you? You thought I meant help out with the actual creatures.'

'No,' he lied. 'Your house, your post - fine. I'll do that, no problem. Shall we go?' He glanced at his watch. It was just past half eight and he'd told the kids to be back before 9pm. He didn't fancy trying to explain why a red-haired woman was dragging a bound group of blue splattered creatures through their new house.

With a bit of a struggle, Michael and Hattie, between them, managed to get the pixies down the stairs and into Hattie's car which was parked outside her house. The car was an old-style, yellow mini and, despite the pixies' small stature, there wasn't enough room in the boot for them to go so they were bundled into the back seat instead.

Once the creatures were in and a seatbelt pulled across them, Hattie pushed the front seat back again and closed the door. She and Michael were stood underneath a street lamp and both had streaks of blue paint on their skin and clothes from where they'd come up against the pixies.

'Good job this stuff does come off,' Michael remarked, looking down at the left sleeve of his jumper which had got much of the paint on it.

Hattie smiled at him. 'Well, thanks for your help, neighbour.'

'I would say "anytime", but...' he replied, in jest.

She took no offence at this. 'I'll maybe see you around, then.' She opened the car door again and slid into the driver's seat. Michael came round and leant an arm over the door frame, and looked down at her.

'You're driving all the way to Devon tonight?' he asked.

'No time like the present,' Hattie said breezily, fishing the car keys from her pocket. She took off the hat Michael had grabbed from the bannister on their way down the stairs, and flung it onto the passenger seat next to her. 'Besides, if I keep them in the house tonight, they'll only keep me awake with their swearing and grumbling. Unless, of course, you have them for the night. We can easily put them back in the attic.' Michael must have looked alarmed at this. Hattie laughed and shook her head. 'Just teasing. No, these guys are best off away from here. Thanks again, Michael.'

'That's quite all right,' Michael replied, stepping away

as Hattie pulled the door closed. Giving him a little wave, she started up the car and drove off. Michael watched until the mini disappeared from view and then he casually walked back into the house, still getting his head around these past few hours.

Tom, Ben and Ingrid returned just a few minutes after nine, carrying two large boxes of pizza. Ingrid had a big bottle of lemonade cradled in her arms. They found Michael sitting in the kitchen, on his laptop, sipping a coffee.

'Hello, you lot,' he said, turning in his stool and smiling at his children. 'So how was Edinburgh?'

'Great!' Ben exclaimed, opening one of the pizza boxes and taking out a slice of what looked like ham and pineapple topping. 'We walked along Princes Street then went bowling. I won, of course.'

'Once,' Ingrid, the youngest of Michael's children, corrected her brother. 'Tom won three times.'

'Ah, but you nearly beat me,' Tom said, tickling his little sister under the chin and making her giggle. 'Thought you'd be hungry, dad, so we got pizza.'

'So I see,' said Michael. The smells were making his mouth water. He dismounted the stool and retrieved some plates from a cardboard box sitting next to the sink. 'And you're right, I'm famished.'

'Did you enjoy your peace and quiet while we were away?' Tom asked, pouring the lemonade into four tumblers. 'Bet you had a nice, boring evening.'

Michael glanced at the laptop screen which was showing an article about pixies, complete with an illustration of the creatures. 'Yes,' he went on, taking a tumbler from his son, 'nice and boring.'

THE END

\#

TEARS OF GOLD

(Edinburgh Elementals)

By Gayle Ramage

Copyright 2013, Gayle Ramage

This story is a work of fiction. The names, characters, places and incidents are products of the writer's imagination or have been used fictitiously. Any resemblance to persons, living or dead, actual events, locales or organisations is entirely coincidental.

As the clock on the office wall heralded the end of another working day, the staff in the Accounts department of Halpin, Green and Buckley, one of the larger law firms in the Scottish capital, started to trickle out of the open-plan office. Most thoughts were on the night ahead where many of them would be spending their time, and money, in the pubs and clubs in nearby Grassmarket, it being the last Friday of the month and, thus, pay day. Cheryl Millican was one of the last to leave as she logged off her computer and waited for it to shut down. She put on her coat draped around her chair, and lifted her handbag from beneath the desk. Someone passed her on the way out and asked if she'd changed her mind about coming for a drink. Cheryl smiled apologetically and shook her head. She had other plans that evening, plans that needed a clear, sober head.

Her flat in the Dalry area of the city was only a fifteen minute brisk walk in the autumnal climate so she had plenty of time for a leisurely shower and some dinner before readying herself for the night ahead.

The house had been chosen by the usual method: A map of Edinburgh spread out on the kitchen table, a closing of the eyes and then the random dropping of an index finger onto the map. She'd visit the chosen street the next day and case the area, picking the building that seemed of most value. When Cheryl had first come to this street, a few days earlier, one of the houses had immediately caught her attention. It didn't look exactly prosperous compared to its neighbours but Cheryl just had a good feeling that she would be foolish to ignore. As if to prove she had made the right decision, Cheryl had spotted the owner of the house - a young red-headed woman - left the house with a suitcase, as if departing for a weekend break somewhere. The house would be empty. Cheryl would not need to rush.

The actual break-in had been very simple, laughably simple, in fact. A window on the first floor landing was left open just enough for Cheryl to slip her latex-gloved fingers through and raise the old, wooden frame. Once she'd climbed through, thankful there were no tricky tables or suchlike making her descent awkward, she took out the flashlight from the rucksack on her back and headed up the stairs to the third floor. As Cheryl moved through the rooms of the house, realisation dawned that she had been right to go with her gut feeling about coming here. The place was chock full of interesting and exotic items and artefacts. Many were locked in display cabinets but that didn't deter Cheryl. She only felt sorry that she couldn't take everything she wanted.

It was in the bathroom, of all places, that she caught sight of the necklace. Of course she'd had no intention of looking through this room, not expecting to find anything worth stealing. But it was the glow from the piece of jewellery, reflecting the city lights coming in from the bathroom window, that forced her attention. As she stepped into the lino-floored room, she discovered that, just like the other treasures, this necklace was contained in a glass case. It sat on a short wooden shelf above an old-fashioned bath tub with brass taps on the end. Cheryl bit her lip and shone the torch over the bathtub. There was no way she could successfully lean over the tub and fiddle with the casing. She would have to step into the bath.

The owner had used plenty of bubble bath, judging by the amount of soap suds clinging to the white enamel, so Cheryl was careful not to slip as she climbed aboard. Steadying herself, she took her rucksack from her shoulders and unzipped it to take out her tools. But then she paused and regarded the glass, narrowing her eyes as she mused upon the same instinctive feeling she'd had when choosing the house. Raising her fingers to the glass box, she gently pulled on the lid. To her surprise, the front panel swung open without a fuss.

Idiot, she thought as she carefully took the long neckwear out, never make it easy for us thieves.

Gripping the necklace in her left hand, she cautiously climbed out of the bath again before having a good look at it with the flashlight. It reminded Cheryl of a necklace she'd once seen in a painting, being worn by some old goddess; all glistening gold with a rotund piece of amber set into the middle of it. As she gazed at the gold, Cheryl decided she would keep this one for herself. Obviously wear it underneath her clothing when around others. The rest of her haul would be sold on, as usual. Eventually, she tore her gaze away from the necklace, placing it into the rucksack with the other items, and continuing with the burglary.

The flashlight zipped around the living room as Cheryl walked in, noting all the bohemian-style rugs, furniture and art around the place. If truth be known, it wasn't a style she liked but her personal tastes never got in the way of a good theft. But before she could begin to rifle through the room for valuables, the unmistakable sound of a door being unlocked echoed in the hallway. Cheryl slipped along to the staircase and climbed the steps. Opening the first floor landing window again, she raised the frame and left the building.

Hattie chucked the brown leather handbag onto the side table next to the front door, relieved to be back home and able to take those bloody heeled shoes off. Not a huge fan of parties, she felt obliged to attend at least one a year, and it being a St Andrew's Day party - despite the event being held a full week before the actual day - she said yes to the RSVP. She headed for the living room and switched the purple-tasseled table lamp on, slumping into the battered-but-comfy orange armchair next to the fireplace. Mere seconds passed before her stomach made her realise she'd not eaten anything at the party. Getting to her feet before she became too settled, she decided to make herself some toast and jam.

'Jesus Christ,' she said, a small echo to her voice as she stood, mouth agape, in the kitchen. If anyone else had been looking into the room they would see nothing untoward. But Hattie saw that the drawer next to the sink wasn't completely closed and that the stainless steel bin by the back door was half an inch more to the left. Someone had

been here. Someone uninvited. Stomach rumblings
ignored, she went to check that nothing had been taken.

An hour later she was sitting on the doorstep, nursing
the hand she'd used to punch the garden's sole tree; a
willow. Things had been taken, though only one of the
stolen items was of any true value: The Brisingamen, a
sparkling gold necklace which had been forged by four
dwarves in ancient times, and that had been displayed in
Hattie's bathroom ever since she'd moved to Edinburgh. As
soon as Hattie had realised the necklace was gone, she'd
calmly went downstairs, left the house and taken out her
stupidity out on the tree trunk. Why the hell had she put the
necklace in the bathroom? The best place to hide
something is in plain sight, a voice from long ago
reverberated in her head.

Hattie stood up to go back inside and put an ice-pack to
her busted hand when someone opened the iron garden
gate. It was Michael and his three children - teenage Tom,
twelve-year-old Ben and seven year old Ingrid. Michael
was leading the way, holding his daughter's hand. Ben was
behind them, peering at Hattie's hand, and Tom was
bringing up the rear, stealing frequent glances at the mobile
phone in his hand.

'Hi,' Michael said. 'Thought I saw someone sitting here.
Locked yourself out?'

'Not quite,' Hattie answered. She gazed down at Ingrid
who was giving her a shy look in return. 'Hello.'

'Hi,' the little girl answered, moving behind her father a
little, in a shy manner.

'Getting settled in Edinburgh, now?'

'What's wrong with your hand?' Ben asked bluntly,
staring at her bloodied knuckles.

'Oh, a tree annoyed me,' Hattie answered, giving the
hand a customary glance. This only made Ben frown.

Michael, used to Hattie and her oddness, seemed

unperturbed. 'We're going to order something from Pizza Hut,' he said. 'You're more than welcome to join us.'

'Dad always orders too much anyway,' Tom added, looking up from the glowing screen of his phone.

Hattie was tempted. She wasn't one to pass up free food and her stomach was making some disturbing-but-quiet noises. But she did have to get that necklace back. Glancing at the house, she said, 'I've been burgled.'

All four faces turned as one to look at her. 'What? When?' Michael asked. 'Are you all right?'

She nodded. 'Yeah, apart from my self-inflicted messed-up hand. They'd gone before I got back.'

'Thought you'd said this area had the lowest crime rate in the city,' Tom muttered to his father, as he finally put the phone in his jacket pocket.

'You've called the police, I assume,' Michael asked, ignoring his son's remarks.

There was a shake of red hair from Hattie. 'No point. You've been in my house. You've seen some of the things I have.' She noted the smirks being exchanged between Michael's sons but said nothing. The children knew nothing about Hattie, other than she was a kind and eccentric woman living across the street. They didn't have a clue about the pixies she and Michael had shifted from his attic, or that Hattie spent more time with giants and forest gods than she did with humans.

'All right,' said Michael, but Hattie could tell he thought she should have rang 999 by now. 'Need a help tidying up?'

'No. Thank you for the offer, though.'

Michael pursed his lips together for a moment then looked at the house. 'Still, I'd like to check that the burglar's still not hanging around. You never know.'

'Aw, our dad the hero,' teased Tom.

'Be my guest,' said Hattie, as she led them into the

house. 'But I'll be fine, I'm sure.'

Once inside, Michael climbed the staircase, telling them he'd start from the top and work his way down. Hattie took the others into the living room to wait. When he'd finished his investigation, his appearance in the living room was accompanied by a look of puzzlement.

'You were actually burgled, weren't you?' he asked, glancing around the tidy room.

Hattie nodded. 'Oh yes.'

'Well,' he said slowly, 'there doesn't seem to be anyone but us lot here. And I've checked the attic.' This last bit drew out a smile from the redhead.

'That's something, I suppose,' she went on to say. 'Something has been taken. A few things, actually, but only one I need to get back.'

'All the more reason to call the police,' said Ben, his gaze fixed on a golden apple sitting solitary on a shelf next to the mantelpiece.

'What is it that you need to get back?' asked Ingrid, almost in a whisper.

'A necklace, sweetie,' Hattie told her. 'A very precious necklace.'

'Sentimental value?' Michael asked.

A pause. 'Yes.' Her belly gurgled loudly at that moment, causing Tom and Ben to snigger. Hattie looked across to Michael, smiling. 'I think that's a yes to your invitation.'

Cheryl caressed the gold chain around her neck as she stared into space. Every time someone passed by her desk, she hid the jewellery beneath her navy blue blouse, and pretended to work. It was foolish to bring the stolen item to work but she couldn't bear not to wear it. Ever since she had slipped it around her neck and fastened the clasp, there was a desire to keep it there, despite the growing sense of unexplainable sadness she felt while wearing it. Even now she could feel the sting of oncoming tears in her eyes. Before she could make a fool of herself in front of her work mates, she shot up from her chair and hurried to the ladies' toilets, making sure her chain was back beneath her clothing again.

Both hands on the edge of the granite sink counter, Cheryl stared at her reflection through water-filled eyes. She was sure the necklace was the cause of this unfathomable sadness; crying and being generally depressed were not things Cheryl normally did or felt. The best thing to do was to let the tears fall and clean the running mascara from her face before returning to the office.

It was while she stood before the row of sinks, weeping, that she heard a brief but gentle noise, like the proverbial pin dropping onto hard flooring. She looked down and, wiping her tear-stained eyes, picked up a small piece of metal; gold, to be precise. She picked it up carefully, wondering if it had fallen from someone's earring or necklace. She'd take it back to the office and ask around, see if it belonged to anyone. Placing it back on the counter for a moment, she went into one of the cubicles, returning moments later with a few sheets of toilet paper to dry her face once she'd washed it. As she turned on the tap and leant towards the mirror, she noticed a tear slowly pass by the corner of her mouth on its way down to her chin. She watched, transfixed, as it reached the curve of her chin and clung on, precariously, for a moment before falling. And that's when Cheryl saw the impossible: the teardrop hit the counter and solidified into gold. It lay mere inches from its twin.

A laugh escaped from Cheryl as she tried to

comprehend what she'd just witnessed. She must have been mistaken. There had been two bits of gold there to begin with and she just hadn't seen the second one, that's all. Another tear was slipping slowly down the side of her nose. Impatiently, she wiped it with a finger and then smeared it onto the counter. Stepping back, her gaze lingered on the surface of the counter. Her mouth grew into a grin at the absurdity of it. Golden tears?

Just to confirm that she wasn't going mad, Cheryl forced herself to think of something utterly heartbreaking until the tears started to flow again. She held her palm out, below her chin to catch the drops. Catching sight of herself in the mirror, she looked ridiculous but, to be honest, she didn't really care. There was no one around to see, and there was a desire to find out just what the hell was going on. When she had worked herself into such a state, with her face blotchy and wet, she was dismayed to find her tears stayed the same, so she took the test again but this time stood over the counter again, her hands by her sides.

When a well-meaning and concerned colleague went to check on Cheryl, they discovered her standing in front of the toilet mirror, laughing manically, with tiny bits of gold dotted around the sinks.

Ten days since the break-in and Hattie was nowhere near getting back the Brisingamen necklace. Contact had been made with those she thought could help, but no one had yet returned with any news. In the meantime there wasn't much she could do. Something she had done, however, on the morning after the burglary, was call upon the city's coven of witches and take them up on their frequent offer of setting up security charms and spells on the house. It was all very Harry Potter and something

Hattie had resisted up until now. She wished for the house to remain as normal as possible, despite some of the more exotic things it contained. But she had been foolish to think the place would be safe, even though the street had the least amount of crime in all of Edinburgh.

That Friday, she sat at a table in The Elephant House on George IV bridge, sipping an iced tea. This had been the place where JK Rowling had written many of the boy wizard's exploits, and thus had become a must-see for tourists. Hattie had been lucky to find a free table.

Two women, both dressed in formal attire, occupied the next table, chatting too much to have their lunch. Hattie couldn't focus on anything but the loudness of their voices, so gave up and listened in. The topic of discussion seemed to be about men, making Hattie wish she'd brought her ipod and earphones along with her. By the time she'd finished her own lunch and was ready to leave, she had intimate knowledge of the women's respective boyfriends: how much sexual prowess they had as lovers, how romantic they were, how much they earned. There had even been talk of how long it would be before the women dumped their beaus for better models. By the way the women were speaking, Hattie hoped the boyfriends would dump them first.

'Oh god, I almost forgot,' said the pale brunette whose hair was in a sleek bob, striped with a dark shade of purple. 'Did you hear about Cheryl Millican?'

'God yeah,' answered her friend, with a gasp. This one was clutching a half-eaten baguette. 'Totally weird, huh? Half the company don't believe it but Alison from Accounts was the one who saw it with her own eyes and she's not someone who'd lie like that.'

Hattie rolled her eyes. These office types were always scandalised over the most trivial things.

'I mean they were definitely gold,' continued the

brunette. 'Harry Cookson swiped a couple of them to get checked out. Definitely gold.'

'Paul reckons she should contact the media. Bet she'd get paid thousands for her story,' said the friend. 'Lucky cow. God, if my tears were gold, I'd be straight to the newspapers.'

Hattie twisted round in her seat and smiled at the two women. 'Sorry, I couldn't help overhearing but did you just say tears of gold?'

The two office workers exchanged looks before the baguette woman leant forward conspiratorially. 'Yes! Someone we work with -'

'Cheryl,' Hattie offered, remembering the name.

'Yeah. Quiet girl. Keeps herself to herself. Aloof, you know. Well, she was found in the ladies toilets at work, crying, with all these tiny gold things everywhere. Someone saw the tears fall and hit the sink, and they turned into gold! How mad is that!'

'The tears turned into gold, she means,' said the brunette. 'Not the person that found Cheryl.'

'Yeah, I gathered that,' said Hattie. 'The counter, was it made from some sort of rock?'

'Granite, I think,' the brunette went on. 'Why?'

'Oh, no reason,' Hattie said cheerfully. She stood and pulled on her brown corduroy jacket. 'I hope your friend Cheryl gets all that she deserves.' She left the cafe and lingered by the bus shelter outside. She presumed the women were on their lunchbreak and would be heading back to their workplace soon. If this Cheryl woman did have the Brisingamen necklace then Hattie would be finding out all she could about the thief, and that meant starting by finding out where she worked.

Some people were the kind to get tired of visitors very quickly and wish their guests could sense this and have the decency to leave shortly afterwards. Cheryl was this kind of person, especially when it came to her sister Natalie. The elder of the two Millican sisters was busy talking or, rather, telling Cheryl what to do, as usual; some idiot at Cheryl's work knew her sister and revealed all about the golden teardrops. As soon as Natalie had heard, she'd come calling.

'I'm just surprised the news hasn't spread,' said Natalie, with a sniff. 'I mean, you cry gold and not one person on Facebook or Twitter mentions it? Sorry, but in this day and age, that's just weird.'

'Not really,' countered Cheryl. 'Only one person saw it with their own eyes, but she didn't film it. There's no proof. Nobody really believes it, anyway.'

'No proof. What about the man who got the tears analysed?' Natalie asked, still grasping the lukewarm cup of tea now forgotten in her hand.

'They could have come from someone's necklace. Again, no proof,' Cheryl replied.

Natalie rolled her eyes and shook her head. 'You're mad not to go to the media about it, that's all I'm saying.'

Yeah, right, thought Cheryl, grumpily.

'Oh, that's new. I've not seen you wear that before.' Natalie was staring at the necklace still hanging around her younger sister's neck. Cheryl had been absently stroking the jewellery while she and her sister had been speaking. Quickly, she put it beneath her jumper again.

'Oh, it's just something I got at a car boot sale ages ago,' she explained before hastily changing the subject.

As the maroon-coloured Lothian bus trundled along the

outskirts of Edinburgh, Hattie discovered she had never
been to this part of the city before. She had lived in the
capital for the best part of ten years and despite it being a
relatively small city, she was still surprised that there were
areas she'd not yet ventured through. The rows of houses
on either side were typical identi-kit affairs; grey slated
roofs, and well-kept gardens. It was like Scotland's version
of the 1950s American Dream home.

Hattie glanced at the back of her left hand where she'd
used a pen to scribble down the number of the house
Cheryl was planning to burgle that night. For over a week
now, Hattie had been following the woman, from work to
home and then out to where she would case prospective
homes to steal from. Last Friday she'd burgled an address
in the New Town. Hattie had waited at the end of the street,
deliberating whether or not to call the police. But before
she'd made up her mind, Cheryl had appeared outside the
house and hot-footed it out of the area. For the past week,
Cheryl had come to this street after work, dressed in a grey
tracksuit and white trainers. She would start jogging as she
turned into the street, then when she reached the soon-to-
be-burgled house, the jogging would cease and Cheryl
would stand looking as if she was out of breath and with a
stitch in her side. Hattie had stood at the corner of a nearby
house, watching this evening ritual.

The house, a thin two-up-two-down, was in total
darkness. Being a Friday night, the occupants were
probably out for the evening. Hattie walked up the garden
path then round the corner to the back door. One of the
Edinburgh witches had given her a charmed key that would
fit in any lock she desired. Pulling the modest-looking key
from her pocket, she paused; she had asked the witch what
good this key would be if the door already had one in the
keyhole. The witch had repeated what she'd originally told
Hattie - the key would work on any door. Here goes

nothing, though Hattie, sliding the key into the lock. So far so good.

Almost half an hour she had been waiting in the living room in the dark, before a noise was heard from the kitchen. Hattie leapt to her feet, panic filling her senses. What if she'd got the wrong house? What if it was the occupiers coming back? She had no magic spells to make her invisible. If it wasn't Cheryl, Hattie would just have to make a run for it.

The door joining the two rooms was wide open so Hattie caught sight of the glow from a flashlight as it ran across the kitchen wall. She froze, her heart racing with adrenalin. Eventually, after a couple of seconds which seemed like hours, the light made its way into the living room, following by a dark figure holding the torch. The light landed on Hattie. It blinded her for a moment but she daren't look away and give Cheryl, if it was she, time to escape.

'Hello, Cheryl,' she said instead, in a casual manner.

The figure stood there, unmoving. Hattie tensed up, ready to make a grab for the thief if she tried to run but Cheryl remained where she was, in the doorway. Wanting to move things forward, Hattie leant across to the light switch on the wall and flicked it on. The figure switched off the torch, pulling off the balaclava with her free hand.

'Who are you?' She finally asked, her cheeks red from the woollen mask. 'You don't live here.'

'Neither do you, though judging by your attire that's pretty much a given,' Hattie said.

'How do you know my name?'

Hattie folded her arms. 'I'm one of your previous victims.'

There was no reaction. Eventually, Cheryl spoke. 'So what are you doing here, then? Oh, wait. Are you trying to be a hero and stop me continuing my dastardly deeds?' she asked, in a mocking voice.

'Well, I wasn't planning to. I'm just here to get back what's mine.'

'Listen, lady, it's not like I always carry around everything I take,' Cheryl snorted. 'I don't exactly keep an inventory of what I steal and from which house.'

'I'll make it easy for you then. There's only one item I want back: The Brisingamen.'

Cheryl made a face. 'What's that, a painting or something?'

Hattie looked directly at the woman. 'It's a necklace. A very special necklace, and I think you know which one I'm talking about.'

Subconsciously the hand not holding the flashlight rose to her throat. 'That's... yours?'

'Not mine exactly. But I'm the curator of it, for the time being,' Hattie said truthfully. 'And you need to give it back. For your own safety.'

'My own safety?' Cheryl laughed at her. 'I don't think I'm in any danger from it. Why should I be worried about my tears turning to gold? Thanks for the concern, though.'

'Yes, yes, I know - Cry upon a rock, your tears become gold. Cry in water and your tears turn to amber. I know what the necklace does,' Hattie said dismissively. 'I'm not talking about the necklace. I'm talking about the people - the creatures - who would be only too happy to bind you to a rock somewhere no one can find you and force you to cry for a long, long time. Just like they did to the last wearer.'

'Oh yeah?' said Cheryl, still with the dubious look in her face. 'And what happened to the last wearer, then? Did their tear ducts dry up? How terrible.'

'He killed himself. Having to wear the necklace for so long eventually drove him suicidal.' Hattie said bluntly. 'His body's in some graveyard in Canada.'

'Yeah, well, tragic story and all that, but if you're not

planning to call the police, would you kindly piss off and leave me to it?'

'Necklace first,' said Hattie, holding out her hand. 'You're wearing it right now, I can see it through your top.'

'Sorry, but I think I'll keep hold of it. You can get it back when I've got enough gold. Hey, I'll even deliver it myself.'

Hattie lowered her hand again. She took off her coat, tossing it onto the leather sofa, and began rolling up her shirt sleeves. It had been a while since she'd fought with anyone, even longer a human.

'What are you doing?' Cheryl managed to say before dropping her rucksack to the ground to ward off the punch Hattie had tried to land on her face.

'You wouldn't listen,' Hattie told her, stepping towards the other woman. 'So I'm taking it back by force.'

Cheryl looked her up and down, laughing bitterly. 'You look like too much of a hippy to be violent.'

Hattie had to agree with the remark. But it didn't stop her swinging her leg back and kicking Cheryl in the shin. The thief toppled to the floor. 'Ow!' Cheryl roared, rubbing her leg. 'That's how you fight, is it? Like a five year old?'

'Why not? You ever been attacked by a five year old?'

Snarling, Cheryl stood up and launched herself at Hattie, aiming for the throat with both hands. Hattie attempted to kick out again but her opponent was ready. Cheryl dodged the kick and took hold of the outstretched leg, twisting it violently. Unfortunately, Hattie wasn't skilled in the ways of ninja-fighting and so crashed into the coffee table, sending a bowl of polished pebbles flying across the room. She jerked her head up in time to see Cheryl swoop down to retrieve her rucksack, intent on leaving.

'Oh no you don't,' Hattie cried, adrenaline helping her to her feet. As Cheryl moved towards the kitchen, Hattie shoved an elbow into her back. The woman stumbled forward and fell through the doorway, smacking her face against the floor. Wasting no time, Hattie straddled Cheryl's back, her fingers scrambling for the top of the polo neck, trying to find the necklace and unclasp it.

'Get off me!' Cheryl shrieked. She wriggled her body wildly from side to side. Her arms flapped behind her, trying to swat Hattie away like a fly. And then fingers found Hattie's long red hair. A hand wrapped itself around a thick strand before Cheryl yanked her arm to the side. Hattie was sent toppling onto the black and white linoleum.

The red head rolled away in time to escape an aimed punch to the stomach, and rose to her knees next to the washing machine. Cheryl aped her movements and they glared at one another, three feet apart, both catching their breath.

'Are you ever going to bloody give up?' Cheryl asked, feeling around her mouth with her fingers. Her top lip was bleeding. 'Jesus, I think you've knocked out a tooth!'

'What, this one?' asked Hattie, holding a small, red smeared molar between her fingers. She'd caught sight of it when the woman had forced her to the floor.

'Oh, thanks. Now I have to go to work missing a tooth,' complained Cheryl.

'My pleasure,' Hattie said, then peered at the tooth. 'Mind you, I could always leave it lying around for the owners to find when they come back. DNA, and all that.' Cheryl lunged forward to grab it but Hattie kept it out of her reach. 'Uh-uh. Necklace first and then you can get your tooth back.'

'Sod off.' Cheryl folded her arms and looked away in disdain.

'Fine,' Hattie shrugged. 'Just expect a nice visit from the police in a day or two.'

Cheryl looked back at her, staring for such a long time, Hattie tensed up, ready to continue the fight. But instead, much to her relief, the thief's shoulders sagged and she took off the necklace. 'You can have the stupid thing back,' she muttered. 'The gold pieces were too small anyway. I'd be in my sixties before I had enough to make me rich.' She tossed the piece of jewellery at Hattie, who caught it with her free hand. True to her word, Hattie duly handed over the tooth which Cheryl slipped into her trouser pocket. 'What now?' Cheryl asked, her breathing returning to normal.

'Well, I'm going home and having a cup of tea, maybe watch a film on TV,' said Hattie, placing the necklace in her bra for safe-keeping. 'Maybe you should do the same. Not my home, though. You've already been there once. And I suggest you stop with the stealing. I've seen your pay slip. I know how much you earn.'

Cheryl's eyes widened. 'How the hell do you know that?'

Hattie smiled and headed towards the back door. 'Really. Stop robbing people.' She opened the door and paused before leaving. She didn't want to say this next bit but she had no option. 'I know where you live, Cheryl. I know a lot about you. And I know some... people... who could make things very uncomfortable for you if you carry on like this. Now you'd best leave soon. You don't want to get caught when you've just turned over a new leaf.' She headed out into the bitter Edinburgh night and decided to make for the nearest bus stop. She wanted to get home as soon as possible and put the necklace under lock and key - and a few spells for good measure.

As the days passed, Hattie received word that Cheryl

had stopped robbing houses in the city, and had become a little paranoid around strangers. Probably thinking they were spies for Hattie. The necklace was back in the bathroom, back in the same glass wall-mounted box, but it had enough charms and spells cast over it to protect it from a nuclear blast. Hattie was putting the rubbish out for the bin collection the next day when she saw Michael come out of his house opposite.

'Did you get your necklace back at all?' he shouted over, heading towards the blue range rover parked on the roadside.

Hattie nodded. 'Oh yes.' She smiled.

'Good. Your hair looks nice like that, by the way.' Even from this distance, she could see his cheeks begin to redden. To save his embarrassment, she patted the mass of red hair piled on top of her head in a big, messy bun.

'Well, hair-pulling can be sore on the old scalp after a while,' she called back.

'Sorry?'

Hattie chuckled and shook her head. 'Doesn't matter.'

THE END

\#
Other Books By The Author

Cigs, Bolan & Strange Men With Guns (Time Travelling
Assassins Prequel #1)
The Shoemaker's Son (Time Travelling Assassins Prequel
#2)
The Whispering Tombs (Quality Times #1)
The Grandparent Trap (Quality Times #2)
The Visitor and Other Stories
Three French Hens - A Christmas Collection

Written as Izzy Hunter

Curiosity Killed

CPSIA information can be obtained at www.ICGtesting.com
Printed in the USA
LVOW08s0301200814

399907LV00001B/198/P